While the city sleeps
in the still of the night,
the white birds of winter
make their flight.

In unwavering lines
they pass by the moon,
whispering their song
from the stars.

A child wakes
to the magical sound.
She counts thousands of birds
southward bound.

Where do they come from?
Where do they go?
These travelers of the night.

They fly from the north
to escape the snows,
from the edge of the earth
where nobody goes,
from the frozen wastes
where the polar bear prowls
and the lone wolf howls to the moon.

The prairies have gone
and machines work the land.
Crops are sown,
grain is grown,
a new landscape is planned.

Then a crack fills the air.
Geese fall to the gun,

twisting and tumbling

one by one.

The survivors move south
to safer ground,

the sound of their voices

drifting down,

waking the children

who want to know....

Where do they come from?
Where do they go?

If they follow the song
of the geese

in full flight

as they pass over cities

and highways

at night,

they will see them come down

in a blizzard of white,

falling like snow

on the lakes

at first light.

As they lift off once more
and circle around

in a rush of wings

and a whirlpool of sound,

they fill the skies

with patterns

and lines,

leading up

leading off

to their wintering grounds.

They head south to the sun
for a season of rest,
to Whispering Water,
a vast wilderness.
A valley of peace in New Mexico
in the ancient land of the Pueblo.

But when the north wind calls
from far away,

the geese become restless;

they know not to stay.

By the moon and the stars

they must find their way

and return to their Arctic home.

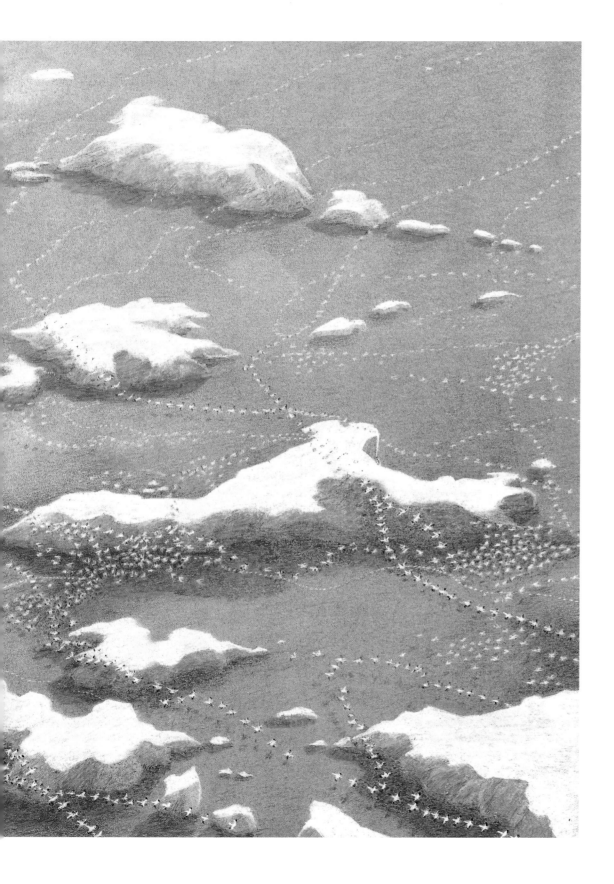

Their song wakes the land
from its long winter sleep.
The sun breaks the ice,
and the ice retreats.

A new year begins,
another cycle complete
in the lives of the migrating geese.

In the melting snow
where the river flows
to the edge of the world
where nobody goes,
the white birds of winter
raise their young
in the land of the midnight sun.

Migration is one of the most awe-inspiring events of the natural world. How can these birds, without compasses or maps, cover such enormous distances? How do they know where they are going?

No one knows for sure, but we have managed to trace their journeys over whole continents. Just as an airplane follows a flight path, it seems that there are flyways for birds, air routes that they follow year after year.

The snow goose is a relentless traveler. The birds nest in the far north of Russia and Canada, and the goslings are hatched during the Arctic summer. Within a few weeks, they have made their first journey with their parents to the tundra wetlands, where there is plenty of food and twenty-four hours of daylight in which to graze. But they do not have much time. Winter arrives early in the north, and soon the snow geese must travel south or starve.

With the arrival of the first snow, the geese take to the air. Some of the Russian birds fly to the north of Alaska and, from there, make a nonstop flight all the way along the Pacific coast to California. As many as two million birds will take the central flyway across the Canadian forests and the farmlands of America, all the way down the eastern side of the Rockies. Tired and hungry, the birds are easy targets for any hunter. Often they fly at night, stopping only briefly for a rest on lakes or wetlands. They fly in a long, straggling line or in a V-shape, taking turns being the leader. Finally, after a journey of nearly three thousand miles, they arrive at their winter homes in California and the Gulf states, and as many as forty thousand birds choose the welcoming reserve of Bosque del Apache, which borders the Rio Grande river in New Mexico. Others will continue even farther south to Mexico.

But they do not rest for long. At the first sign of spring three months later, they take off for the northern skies on another long and dangerous journey to the Arctic to raise a new generation of snow geese.

Today people are trying to help the birds on their journey. They have created new reserves and replaced some of the old watering holes on the migration routes. They have even begun to plant special fields of corn for the birds. Although a fifth of their number are lost to hunters each year, the flocks of snow geese are increasing, and they are able to continue their ancient pattern of migration across America.

**DATE DUE**

| AM-K | | | |
|------|---|---|---|
| PM-K | | | |
| Am-k | | | |
| Pm-k | | | |
| 2 | | | |
| | | | |
| AmK | | | |
| 2 | | | |
| PM-K | | | |
| | | | |